Archie Celebrates DIWALI

Mitali Banerjee Ruths

Illustrated by **Parwinder Singh**

I'm Archana. Everyone calls me Archie.

Charlesbridge

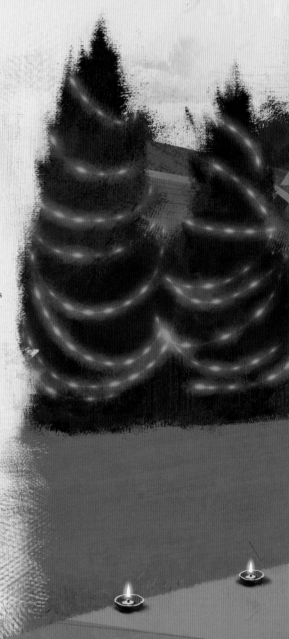

To my wonderful family and the vibrant Texas community who raised me—M. B. R.

To the multilingual and diverse culture of India— where celebrating festivals is an integral part of a healthy and happy social life—P. S.

Text copyright © 2021 by Mitali Banerjee Ruths
Illustrations copyright © 2021 by Parwinder Singh
All rights reserved, including the right of reproduction in whole or in part in any form.
Charlesbridge and colophon are registered trademarks of Charlesbridge Publishing, Inc.

At the time of publication, all URLs printed in this book were accurate and active.
Charlesbridge, the author, and the illustrator are not responsible for the content
or accessibility of any website.

Published by Charlesbridge
9 Galen Street
Watertown, MA 02472
(617) 926-0329
www.charlesbridge.com

Library of Congress Cataloging-in-Publication Data
Names: Ruths, Mitali Banerjee, author.
Title: Archie Celebrates Diwali / Mitali Banerjee Ruths; illustrated by Parwinder Singh.
Description: Watertown: Charlesbridge, 2021. | Summary: "Archie is worried that her
    school friends won't like Diwali, her favorite Hindu holiday, and when a storm knocks
    out the electricity, it looks like the party may be ruined."—Provided by publisher.
Identifiers: LCCN 2019014217 (print) | LCCN 2019981083 (ebook) |
    ISBN 9781623541194 (library binding) | ISBN 9781632898906 (ebook)
Subjects: LCSH: Divali—Juvenile fiction. | Hindu children—Juvenile fiction. |
    Hinduism—Customs and practices—Juvenile fiction. | East Indian Americans—
    Juvenile fiction. | Friendship—Juvenile fiction. | CYAC: Divali—Fiction. |
    Hinduism—Customs and practices—Fiction. | East Indian Americans—Fiction. |
    Friendship—Fiction.
Classification: LCC PZ7.1.R9 Mi 2021 (print) | LCC PZ7.1.R9 (ebook) | DDC
    [Fic]—dc23
LC record available at https://lccn.loc.gov/2019014217
LC ebook record available at https://lccn.loc.gov/2019981083

Printed in China
(hc) 10 9 8 7 6 5 4 3 2 1

Illustrations created digitally in Photoshop with Wacom tablet and pen
Display type set in Blue Liquid by Creativeqube Design
Text type set in Jenson Pro by Adobe Systems Incorporated
Color separations by Colourscan Print Co Pte Ltd, Singapore
Printed by 1010 Printing International Limited in Huizhou, Guangdong, China
Production supervision by Jennifer Most Delaney
Designed by Diane M. Earley

This year Archie invites a few friends from school to her family's big Diwali party. Virgil and Nora say they never heard of Diwali, and Paisley has trouble pronouncing it. Archie worries—what if they don't like her favorite holiday?

Archie rakes the leaves . . . plugs in the lights . . . fixes a smudge in the rangoli . . . and lines up every diya on the walkway.

Everything needs to be perfect, thinks Archie, straightening the garland of paper marigolds.

Archie's family is busy in the kitchen. Krishna makes a mess in his high chair.

Archie tastes Dida's special curry. *Maybe it's too spicy*, she worries.

"For your friends, I put only one chili," says Dida.

"You know the reason we have Diwali every year?" asks Poppy Uncle.

"To celebrate the triumph of good over evil," Archie answers, arranging the sweets.

"Well, yes!" says Poppy Uncle with a wink. "But really it's so your grandmother can sing karaoke!"

Everybody laughs. Archie secretly hopes Dida doesn't sing too much and Poppy Uncle doesn't tell too many jokes in front of her friends.

"Let's get your new clothes on," says Ma.

Archie twirls. She loves the sequins on her lehenga.

"You look like a maharani!" says Ma. "A real Indian queen!"

Archie looks in the mirror. Maybe her friends will think she looks weird. They've never seen her dressed up like this.

The doorbell rings. Archie's heart skips a beat, but it's just Mr. and Mrs. Goldman with a huge umbrella.

It's pouring outside. Leaves litter the lawn. The rangoli is ruined. The diyas are drenched. A marigold garland blows down the street. There are flashes of lightning and rumbles of thunder. It sounds like a demon battle up in the clouds.

"Quite a Diwali downpour!" says Mr. Goldman.

Archie stares at the mess. She and her friends won't get
to play outside. They'll be trapped inside with the grown-ups.
This party is already boring and terrible, Archie thinks.

Archie's friend Seema arrives. She goes to a different school, but she and Archie have known each other since they were babies. "You look nice," says Seema. She isn't wearing Indian clothes. "Thanks," mumbles Archie, tugging at her lehenga. Maybe she should change. She doesn't want to be the only one who looks like a maharani.

But it's too late. Right then her school friends Nora,
Paisley, and Virgil arrive. Archie fidgets with her bangles.
"What's on your forehead?" asks Virgil.
"It's like a sticker," says Archie. "For decoration."
"It's called a bindi," Seema offers.

Just then, Paisley sneezes three times in a row.

And the lights go out.

"You blew out the power!" Virgil says in the darkness.

"Stay calm, everyone!" says Archie's dad. "We have candles, flashlights, and plenty of batteries."

"We can still eat and have a good time!" Archie's mom adds.

"Try a bit of everything," says Dida, handing plates to Archie and her friends.

They sit around a lantern like they're camping.
Paisley squints at her plate. Archie twists a napkin,
waiting for someone to take a bite.

"Burning!" Nora gasps.

"You need mango lassi!" Archie quickly hands her a glass. "It's like tongue lotion. Sorry about the food."

"It's spicy," says Nora. "But good."

"I could eat this yummy pillow bread forever." Virgil stuffs another piece into his mouth.

"That's naan," Archie explains with a tiny smile.

"So what's Diwali about?" asks Paisley.

"Um, it's the Festival of Lights," says Archie, picking at the sequins on her skirt. *And we have no lights*, she thinks. *Worst Diwali party ever.*

"So . . . Diwali is about lights?" says Nora. "That's it?"

Everybody waits. Archie's face gets warm. She takes a deep breath.

"A long time ago this king and queen saved the world from a whole bunch of demons," Archie begins. "Then they tried to find their kingdom, but it was super dark, and nobody had electricity."

"Like right now," whispers Virgil.

"Shh!" Nora and Paisley say at the same time.

Archie continues, "The people didn't know if the king and queen would find their way, so they lit thousands of little oil lamps. . . ."

Her friends lean in and listen so closely that Archie feels shy. Her voice trails off.

"So what happened?" asks Paisley.

"Did demons chase them?" asks Virgil.

Archie shakes her head. "Nope. The king and queen made it home safely. Everybody lived happily ever after."

"Now every fall, on the night of a new moon . . ." adds Seema.

Archie finishes, "We celebrate Diwali to remember that evil and darkness can't win against all our lights shining together."

Suddenly the power comes back on. Paisley squeals. Nora cheers. Virgil drops his naan. The adults all clap.

Archie smiles. "Wow! Perfect timing!"

"Diwali miracle!" shouts Poppy Uncle. He turns up the music and hands Dida the microphone.

Virgil taps his foot to the beat.

Nora turns to Archie. "Can I have a bindi?"

"Me, too?" asks Seema.

"Sure!" says Archie with a huge grin. "I have lots!"

Mr. and Mrs. Goldman show off their Bollywood moves. Ma and Krishna start a conga line. Archie and her friends join in. They go around the living room, through the kitchen, and out to the patio.

The rain has stopped. The grass glistens. Lanterns twinkle in the trees. Everyone lights sparklers under the night sky.

Archie covers her ears when her dad sets off firecrackers.
"Scare away those evil spirits!" Poppy Uncle shouts.
The loud noises also scare baby Krishna.
"I've never eaten or danced so much in my life!" Paisley cries.

It's getting late. Everyone gets ready to go. Dida brings containers of food. "I packed extra naan for you," Dida whispers to Virgil.

"I love your whole family!" says Nora.

Archie smiles. She loves her whole family, too.

"I'm so glad you all came," says Archie.

Maybe next year, she thinks, *I'll hand out more invitations at school.*

Ma tucks Archie in. "Good night, maharani!"
Archie touches the bindi on her forehead and smiles.
"Happy Diwali!" she says.

MORE ABOUT ARCHIE'S FAVORITE HOLIDAY

Diwali, the festival of lights, comes from India and is now celebrated in many countries, such as the United States, Canada, the United Kingdom, and Australia. The festival lasts five days, and the main celebration takes place on the very dark night of the new moon between October and November. There are many mythical stories about the origins of Diwali, like ancient warriors defeating powerful demons, but at their heart, all the stories are about how good triumphs over evil. There are also many different ways of celebrating Diwali, just as there are many different ways of celebrating other holidays around the world. People usually wear new clothes, gather with friends and family, and decorate their homes with lights.

The Story of the Ramayana

One of the most popular Diwali stories comes from the *Ramayana*, an epic poem written thousands of years ago in an ancient language called Sanskrit. *Ramayana* means "Rama's journey." It tells the story of a prince named Rama who has to rescue his wife, Sita, after she gets kidnapped by a ten-headed demon king named Ravana. Rama gets help from his brother and a monkey-king named Hanuman. To help Rama and Sita find their kingdom again, people light hundreds of tiny lanterns to guide them home. When they return, they are crowned king and queen. They rule for many years over their kingdom in peace with no more evil demons bothering anyone.

GLOSSARY

Decorations

diya—An oil lamp made from clay, now often used with tea lights or electric candles to decorate homes for Diwali.

rangoli—An art form with circular patterns, usually with repeating geometric and floral shapes, created on floors or courtyards for decoration and good luck using materials such as colored sand, rice, flour, petals, or chalk.

garland—A strand of flowers, usually bright marigolds, often used to decorate doorways for special occasions.

Food

curry—A dish of meat or vegetables prepared in a thick sauce with a complex combination of Indian spices.

naan—An oven-baked flatbread, usually served hot and brushed with butter, used to scoop other foods like dal or curry.

sweets—A general term for desserts made with sugar and milk or condensed milk, often with nuts like almonds or pistachios, and sometimes decorated with actual gold or silver leaf.

mango lassi—A cold, soothing drink made with mango and yogurt.

Clothing and Accessories

sari—A long piece of cloth, often beautifully woven and embroidered, wrapped around a woman's waist with one end draped over a shoulder. Saris are usually worn with a fitted blouse and petticoat, and different regions of India have different draping styles; worn by Archie's grandmother in the story.

salwar kameez—Long baggy trousers worn with a long tunic shirt that usually reaches below the knees; worn by Archie's mother in the story.

lehenga—A long, heavily embroidered skirt worn at weddings, traditional parties, or folk dances, with a fitted blouse that leaves the midriff bare.

sherwani—A long coat-like garment made with heavier fabric and lining, worn by men for weddings and other special occasions; worn by Archie's dad and uncle in the story.

bangles—Matching sets of bracelets worn on each arm.

bindi—Traditionally a red dot of vermilion powder worn on the center of the forehead close to the eyebrows. Ornamental bindis now come in different shapes and colors as sheets of little stickers.

Other

maharani—A title from Sanskrit—an ancient language of India—meaning "great queen."

Bollywood—A nickname for India's Hindi-language film industry based in the city of Mumbai, formerly known as Bombay (Bollywood = Bombay + Hollywood). The movies often have elaborate song-and-dance numbers made from a fusion of many genres, from folk to disco to hip-hop.

dida—"Grandmother" in Bengali—a language Archie's family speaks—specifically a mother's mother.

MAKE YOUR OWN DIYAS

On Diwali, people around the world light millions of diyas. Traditionally they're little oil lamps made out of clay, but you can make your own diyas to use with a tea light or small battery-powered candle. Always get help from an adult before using the oven.

Prep time: 20 minutes | Cook time: about 3 hours | Yield: 4 to 5

You'll need:

- a large bowl
- a small bowl
- 2 disposable mixing spoons
- 2 cups of flour
- 1 cup of salt
- ½ cup of water

- ½ cup of acrylic paint, any color
- various gems, glitter, beads, or sequins
- a cookie sheet
- small tea lights or battery-powered candles
- optional: nontoxic varnish, like Mod Podge or PVA glue, and a brush

1. In the large bowl, mix together the flour and salt.

2. In the small bowl, mix together the water and paint.

3. Slowly add the water-paint mixture from the small bowl to the flour-salt mixture in the large bowl. Knead the mixture until it becomes a smooth dough. You may not need all of the water-paint. If the dough gets too sticky, add a little more flour.

4. Roll the dough into four or five 3-inch balls. Press your thumbs into the center of each one to make a spot big enough to fit a tea light or candle. (But don't put the lights in yet!)

5. Decorate your diyas with gems, glitter, beads, or sequins.

6. Place them on an ungreased cookie sheet and bake in the oven at 200 degrees Fahrenheit for about 3 hours, until hardened.

7. Optional: Once the diyas have cooled, brush them with nontoxic varnish like Mod Podge or PVA glue to seal. (This isn't required, but it will make your diyas shiny!)

8. Place your tea lights or candles in the diyas. Let them shine in the dark.

For more Diwali crafts and activities, visit www.mitaliruths.com.